FAMOUS ANIMAL STORIES

SNOWFOOT

White Reindeer of the Arctic

By Justin F. Denzel

Illustrated by Taylor Oughton

GARRARD PUBLISHING COMPANY
CHAMPAIGN, ILLINOIS

SNOWFOOT

White Reindeer of the Arctic

A bright noon sun warmed the Arctic tundra as Taku the Lapp boy looked at the newborn reindeer. In all his eleven years, Taku had never seen such a beautiful white fawn.

Only a few minutes before, he had found the young mother reindeer lying on her side, struggling to give birth. Speaking in a quiet voice, Taku reached down. He patted the doe softly to ease her fears. Then, with gentle, knowing hands, Taku helped bring the little fawn into the world.

The dark eyes of the newborn animal opened wide. Taku was the first living thing the little reindeer saw.

Now, standing a few feet away, Taku watched as the mother reindeer licked the young one clean. A few moments later the fawn tried to get up. But he was weak and unsteady.

Taku reached down to help. This time a strong hand held him back. It was the hand of his father, Mangus Bokar.

"Let it be," said the old herdsman. "It is her firstborn. She must learn to take care of it herself."

A short while later the fawn was able to walk. He followed his mother to the hillside where the other reindeer were grazing.

Mangus Bokar saw the look in his son's eyes. "You would like to have the little one for your own," he said.

Taku looked up. "I would be willing to give three of my deer for so fine a calf."

Mangus Bokar tried to hide his smile. "That will not be necessary," he said. "When the time comes we will mark the fawn with your sign."

Taku was very happy. He already had eleven animals, one for each year. The white fawn would be the finest one of all.

As he walked along the hillside, tending the reindeer, Taku looked out across the brown meadow. It spread like a carpet to the edge of the Arctic Sea. Here his father's herd of reindeer would graze all summer.

Taku loved this Finnish northland. It had rugged hills and many beautiful fjords that echoed to the wild call of the loon. It was Taku's home. He knew no other.

As soon as his work was over, he ran down the hill to the family camp. There he told his mother about the fawn.

She smiled, showing her white teeth against clear bronze skin. "I am happy for you," she said.

"You must see him," said Taku.

"I will see him soon enough," said his mother. She turned back to her cooking. "Go," she said, "and tell your sister."

Taku raced across the camp. "Inka, Inka," he shouted.

A dark head poked out from one of the tents. "You sound like an angry walrus," said Inka.

"No," said Taku, "I am happy. I have a new fawn."

Inka smiled. "Another so soon?"

"Yes," said Taku, "a white one. Come and see."

Together they ran up the hill. Their reindeer boots pushed through the thick meadow grass. Their deerskin jackets were trimmed with bright colors of red and yellow.

When they reached the top, they found the reindeer still grazing along the hillside. A number of small shaggy dogs ran about, keeping the herd together.

At the edge of the herd, Taku saw the white fawn standing with his mother. "There," he said.

The little fawn came close to Taku without fear.

"I have never seen a fawn do that before," said Inka.

"That is because I was there when he was born," said Taku. "He will not forget."

Taku and Inka petted the little fawn. They liked the soft, silky feel of his fluffy white fur. They laughed and giggled when he sucked on their fingers.

When it was time for them to go, the fawn did not want to be left behind. He followed them down the hill.

"Maybe you can keep him in your tent," said Inka.

But when Taku asked his father, the old man shook his head. "The new fawn belongs with the herd," he said. "It is not good to make him a pet. If you keep him here, he will not learn to take care of himself."

"But you have old Ringar," said Taku.

"Ringar is one of our work animals," said his father. "He helps pull our sleds and carry our belongings. Of what use would your fawn be around camp?"

Taku threw back his shoulders. "When Snowfoot grows up he too will pull a sled."

Taku's father looked at him. "I see you have already given him a name."

"Yes," said Taku. "He is white, but the fur around his hooves is the whitest of all."

But Mangus Bokar was firm. "There is much work to do," he said. "You will not have time to take care of the fawn. Tomorrow you must take him back to his mother."

The next morning Taku put the little fawn on his shoulders and carried it up into the hills. He found the mother grazing near the edge of the herd. He put the little one down beside her.

That afternoon, as Taku tended the herd, he heard a low mournful howl. It came from the north. When he told his father about it, the old man nodded. "Yes, the wolves are back," he said. "They always seem to know when there are many calves. We will have to watch closely tonight."

That evening Taku went out to keep his nightly watch. His father tended the far side of the herd. Taku watched the side nearest camp.

But the wolves were wise. They came in where the herdsman did not expect them. Taku knew the wolves had come when he saw the herd moving about. He could hear the mother reindeer grunting, calling the calves to their sides. The dogs barked and raced about, trying to keep the herd together.

Quickly Taku made his way around the frightened animals. They pushed and kicked to get as far away from the danger as possible.

When Taku reached the spot where the wolves had been, his father was already there. The wolves had carried off three calves.

"They are bold with hunger," said Taku's father. "It will be best if we move the herd into the valley."

They began to drive the herd down the hillside. As they moved along Taku looked around for Snowfoot. He had not gone far when he caught a glimpse of something white lying in the grass. He ran over to look at it more closely. His heart sank. It was Snowfoot, and he was badly hurt.

The fawn looked up at him with dark, pleading eyes.

Mangus Bokar watched as his son bent over Snowfoot. "The little one was knocked down during the panic," he said. "His leg is broken."

Taku lifted the fawn and held him in his arms.

"What are you going to do with him?" asked his father.

"I am going to take care of him," said Taku. "Maybe I can make him well again."

"No," said his father. "The animal's leg is broken. You cannot fix it. You must kill him."

Taku looked away. He knew that an injured animal should be killed. But he could not make himself do away with Snowfoot. "I cannot do that," he said.

"But you must," said Mangus Bokar, firmly. "We can make boots from the skin. The meat will feed the dogs."

Taku knew his father spoke the truth. Herding reindeer was a hard life. The herdsman had to make use of everything around him. He must waste nothing.

Still, Taku could not kill the fawn. He started down the hill with the little deer in his arms.

His father called after him. "You will

have to do as I say," he shouted. "You cannot waste your time taking care of an injured animal."

All night long Taku sat in his tent. He held Snowfoot in his lap and fed him milk from a deerskin pouch.

The next morning his mother came. "Your father is angry," she said. "Why do you not do as he wishes?"

"Because I cannot kill Snowfoot," said Taku.

Taku's mother shook her head sadly. "It is not the first time we have killed a fawn."

"But Snowfoot is different," said Taku. "Someday he will be a fine, strong bull—if only I can find a way to fix his broken leg."

Taku's mother sat beside her son. "My grandmother once healed the broken leg of a young doe," she said.

Taku looked up, a bit of hope shining in his eyes. "Do you think we can do it again?"

"I don't know," said his mother. "We can try."

Mrs. Bokar went out into the fields. She returned with a handful of willow sticks. First she wrapped the little fawn's leg in deerhide. Over this she placed the willow sticks. Then she bound the sticks with strips of sealskin.

When she had finished she stood up. "Now," she said, "I must go tell your father what I have done. He will not be pleased."

Taku waited. He knew that his mother would speak for him. But he wondered if his father would listen.

That afternoon his mother came to the tent again. "Your father wishes to see you," she said.

Taku ran up into the hills, where his father was tending the herd. His heart beat fast. His father did not even look at him as he came near.

"The fawn still lives," said Taku.

"Against my wishes," said his father.

"I am sorry," said Taku. "But I just cannot kill the little one."

"Do you understand?" asked Taku.

"I understand that you are a foolish boy," said Mangus Bokar. "I understand too that you must learn a lesson."

Taku waited. He was sure his father was going to punish him.

"You will keep the fawn," his father went on. "You will take care of him and make him well if you can."

Taku could hardly believe what his father was saying.

"It will take a lot of work," his father said. "It will not be easy. At the same time you will tend the herd. You will help your mother. You will do all your other work too. And you will learn what it means to care for an injured animal."

Taku was happy. He was willing to do all these things and more. He thanked his father and told him he would do his work as well as ever.

Mangus Bokar looked straight ahead. "I have not finished," he said.

Taku waited.

"How long will it be before you take the wrappings off the fawn's leg?" asked his father.

"Mother says the leg will heal quickly. Maybe by the end of summer."

"By then the herd will be ready to move south," said his father.

"Yes," said Taku.

The old herdsman looked at his son for the first time. His eyes were hard. "If the fawn cannot walk by that time, you must kill him."

Taku held his breath. He knew his father meant what he said.

There was a long silence.

"Then it is agreed?" said his father.

Taku looked at the ground. He had no other choice. He almost choked as he said the words. "Yes, it is agreed."

Week after week Taku took care of Snowfoot. Many times each day he milked the reindeer cows to get milk for the little fawn.

At the same time Taku did his work. He tended the herd for many hours each night. During the day he helped his mother around camp. He gathered wood and picked cloudberries. Often he went without sleep. It was not easy to care for the injured fawn.

Yet in spite of the extra work, Taku did not give up. He fed the fawn well. Over the weeks he watched him grow.

When Snowfoot started to eat by himself, Taku took him along as he tended the herd. Snowfoot walked about on unsteady legs. Secretly Taku wondered if he would ever run again.

The summer days passed quickly. The rooks began to gather in the pine trees. Long lines of snow geese flew overhead.

Soon the snow started to fall in the valley.

A few days later the tents were taken down. Then Mangus Bokar harnessed old Ringar to the lead sled.

Taku and Inka helped their mother tie up the household belongings. They loaded them on the sleds.

A short while later the reindeer began moving south.

Mangus Bokar looked at his son. Taku knew the time had come. He untied the bindings on Snowfoot's leg. The young fawn tried to walk. But he stumbled and fell to his knees.

Taku held his breath. "Walk, Snowfoot, walk," he begged. The calf stood up again. He was frightened and uncertain. Each time he took a step he fell.

Taku's heart felt like a stone in the bottom of his stomach. He saw his father coming toward him. He had a long hunting knife in his hand. The blade flashed in the sun. He held it out to Taku. "Take it," he said. "We will go ahead. You know what you have to do."

Taku took the knife in his hand. He wanted to say no. Yet he did not dare to disobey.

Taku watched as his family went down the trail and disappeared into the trees. He looked around at the empty campsite. Now it would be a place of

sadness. He would never want to return.

Taku held Snowfoot close. In his other hand he held the knife. It would only take a moment. Then it would be over.

Then Taku knew that it would never be over. He would always remember the moment for the rest of his life.

Without thinking he dropped the knife to the ground. He started to run. He ran as fast as he could. Maybe Snowfoot would find his way south, he thought. Maybe he would meet up with the herd. Then he would be safe. Yet, even as he thought this, he knew he was wrong.

He saw an eagle circling high in the sky. He knew that soon it would find the injured calf. Or perhaps the wolves would find him first.

The thought made Taku turn back. He had only gone a few steps when he heard the sound of running feet.

A moment later Snowfoot came racing through the trees. He ran up to Taku and licked his hand. At first Taku was surprised. Then he knew what had

happened. The fawn's leg had been bound up for weeks. It was stiff and unsteady. That was why Snowfoot could not walk at first. Now he could walk as well as any reindeer in the herd.

Taku went back and got the knife. Now he would not have to use it. Then happily he followed the winding trail of the sleds. Snowfoot walked gracefully by his side.

Taku soon caught up with his family as they followed their reindeer. Three weeks later they reached the cabins and log huts in the middle of the forest. Here they would spend the winter.

Taku's father was not happy when he saw that the young fawn could walk.

"The animal is useless," he insisted. "His care will take up much time that might be used for better things."

"I will turn him back to the herd," said Taku. "Then he will learn to take care of himself."

But the fawn had been away too long. The man scent was strong on his body. The herd did not want him. Twice Taku had to save him from the attacks of the young bulls.

And so Taku continued taking care of his pet deer. He had to see that he had food each day. He had to teach him to find water. He had to watch over him so he would not be caught by the wildcats and wolves. 1925839

For two years Snowfoot followed Taku and his family back and forth on their yearly travels. During that time he grew in size and beauty. Each year, in the summer, his new antlers grew larger. His coat was a thick, fluffy white. Now he was a magnificent full-grown bull.

But Taku's father still thought of him as nothing more than a useless pet. "That fine white coat of his would be worth more as a jacket or a pair of boots," he said.

"Someday Snowfoot will be the finest deer in the herd," Taku replied.

Mangus Bokar looked hard at his son. "Soon you will be going away to school. Who will look after Snowfoot then?"

Taku had almost forgotten that he was going to school. In a few weeks he and Inka would leave for the state school. It was two hundred miles away. Who would take care of Snowfoot?

The next day Taku was tending the herd. He watched the young bulls as they played at fighting. They jumped about, pushing each other with their antlers.

Suddenly Taku knew what he must do. He must train Snowfoot. He must teach him to fight and defend himself.

That afternoon Taku put on his skis and took Snowfoot out into the clearing. Using an old pair of antlers, he ran and jabbed at the young deer.

At first Snowfoot was frightened. He could not understand this new game. Then suddenly he knew what to do. He lowered his head and jabbed back. Taku was happy that Snowfoot learned so quickly. Then, with Inka's help, Taku made a good, strong harness. He taught Snowfoot how to pull a sled.

When Snowfoot was trained Taku took him out once more and left him with the herd. But the next morning Snowfoot came back. His white coat was covered with mud and dirt. He had defended himself well. But he was no match for the dozens of old bulls who drove him out of the herd.

Taku was very sad. He could think of nothing more to do.

A few days later Taku's father hitched old Ringar to a sled. He went to the village to trade furs for coffee and sugar.

While he was gone it started to snow. Soon there was an icy blizzard. Mrs. Bokar began to worry.

"I will go to meet him," said Taku. "He may still be in the village waiting for the storm to end."

Taku hitched Snowfoot to a sled. The snow was still falling when he left, but soon the storm ended. Like magic the sky changed from dark gray to gold. A

40

beautiful glow of bright colors spread across the heavens. It was the northern lights.

But Taku had little time to enjoy their beauty as he urged Snowfoot on. Then Taku heard the familiar howl of the wolves in the distance. He reached down and touched the hunting knife fastened to his belt.

A few minutes later he came to an open valley. There he saw the wolves outlined against the snow. They were standing in a wide circle. And in the center was a man fighting for his life.

Quickly Taku ordered Snowfoot on. As he drew near Taku gasped. The man in the circle was his father. Old Ringar lay at his feet.

The wolves drew back as Taku jumped out of the sled. He held his knife in one hand.

Taku's father was tired and out of breath. "The wolves have followed us all afternoon," he said. "Old Ringar could run no further. He died in the harness."

The wolves came back now, snapping and growling. Taku and his father fought bravely. They jabbed and slashed with their knives.

Then Taku heard a wild howl. He turned in time to see Snowfoot tossing one of the wolves high into the air.

Taku's father could hardly believe what he saw. "Cut him loose," he shouted. "He will have a better chance."

Quickly Taku's knife flashed as he cut Snowfoot out of the harness. Now the young bull was free to fight as he chose. Savagely he rushed and jabbed.

Taku and his father stood on either side of the white reindeer and protected his flanks and rear. They fought on, minute after minute. Snowfoot's antlers found their mark again and again. To Taku it seemed as though the battle would never end.

Then the wolves started to tire. The great white deer was too much for them. They were angry and sullen as they broke off the fight.

When it was over Snowfoot stood tall and brave. Taku was proud of his big white reindeer.

Taku and his father buried old Ringar in the snow. Then Taku put Ringar's harness on Snowfoot and hitched him to the sled. He helped his father climb in and covered him up with the deerskin blanket. Under the bright glare of the northern lights, they started for home.

A few days later Taku was in the family cabin getting his things ready for school. Today he was leaving home. Most of all, he was leaving Snowfoot.

He could hear his father, who was loading the sleds. Then he heard him call, "Come, Taku, it is time to go. Inka is waiting."

Slowly Taku picked up his belongings. As he opened the door and looked out, he stopped in surprise. A happy smile crossed his face.

There was Snowfoot dressed in a new harness, trimmed in reds and greens. He was hitched to the lead sled.

Taku's father grinned. "We need a new lead reindeer," he said. "I think Snowfoot will do just fine."

Taku smiled as he waved good-bye to his mother. He knew that in a few months he would be coming home. When he did, Snowfoot would be there waiting for him.